SQUIRREL on STAGE

SQUIRREL on STAGE

by **Vivian Vande Velde**

illustrated by
Steve Björkman

HOLIDAY HOUSE · New York

Library of Congress Cataloging-in-Publication Data
Names: Vande Velde, Vivian, author. | Björkman, Steve, illustrator.
Title: Squirrel on stage / by Vivian Vande Velde ; illustrated by Steve Björkman.
Description: First edition. | New York : Holiday House, [2022] | "An 8
class pets + 1 squirrel book" | Audience: Ages 7–10 | Summary:
"A schoolyard squirrel and Pet Rat try to watch the student production
Cinderella but end up stealing the show when they accidentally
end up on stage"— Provided by publisher.
Identifiers: LCCN 2021042675 | ISBN 9780823452156 (hardcover)
Subjects: CYAC: Squirrels—Fiction. | Rats—Fiction. | Theater—Fiction.
Schools—Fiction. | Humorous stories. | LCGFT: Animal fiction.
Humorous fiction.
Classification: LCC PZ7.V3986 Sqs 2022 | DDC [Fic]—dc23
LC record available at https://lccn.loc.gov/2021042675

ISBN: 978-0-8234-5215-6 (hardcover)

Dedicated to all the teachers who—with everything else they have to do—decide to help their students put on a play. —V.V.V.

Contents

Twitch:
The Schoolyard Squirrel

Squirrels tell the best stories. Wonderful squirrel stories
I have heard include:

- *adventures* such as "My Death-Defying Escape from
  a Cat,"
- *tragedies* such as "Uncle Whiskers Drops a French
  Fry and Watches as a Seagull Steals It Away,"
- *romances* such as "How Your Father and I Met in a
  Trash Can,"
- and *comedies* such as "Nearsighted Cousin Chatter
  Mistakes a Lawn Ornament for Her Brother."

I have a very interesting story of my own about the time I buried a whole bunch of acorns, and then I couldn't remember where I'd put them, and then I found them again. I guess that would be a *mystery* story.

I learned the names of the different kinds of stories because I live in the yard that's part of the people school, and because I'm an excellent listener.

I love all kinds of stories.

Chipmunks' stories tend to be short and jokey.

Groundhogs' stories are very long with lots and lots of characters who can be hard to keep track of.

And moles' stories often start out making you laugh but usually you're crying by the end.

My least favorite are bird stories. Bird stories are very limited. They're mostly: "This is my berry. Go away and leave me alone." Or: "This is my worm. Go away and leave me alone." Not much in the way of character or plot or suspense *there*. Birds are limited in their thinking. They

even believe the seeds people put in the squirrel feeders are for *them*. The birds don't notice the rides people build around the feeders: the slippery poles, the wobbly disks, the roofs that we have to dangle upside down from in order to get to the food—a playground, all for squirrels' amusement, because squirrels are not limited in their thinking.

Sometimes I'm in the mood for one kind of story, sometimes another.

On this afternoon, I'm feeling a bit lazy. I've just eaten a nice juicy piece of peach a person threw away (people are always throwing away perfectly good food so that squirrels can have a well-rounded change from the seeds in all those squirrel feeders), and I'm thinking: *My tummy is full, so I don't need food. It's not cold or raining or too windy—so I don't need shelter.*

What I need is a story.

No other squirrels are around at the moment, so that means I won't hear the best-possible story.

I don't see any mice. Mice are close cousins to squirrels, so their stories are similar to squirrel stories. But mice are terrible storytellers. They're always interrupting each other, and talking over each other, and they have trouble remembering important details, so someone is always going, "Oh, wait! I forgot to tell you . . ."

There's a chipmunk nearby, but she caught sight of the peach at the same moment I did, only with her shorter legs, I got to it first. I don't think I want to hear any story she might choose to tell at this point.

Living in a schoolyard, I sometimes listen to the people children tell each other stories while they are on the playground. But it's been a while since I heard the ringing of the bell that says the school day is over.

And yet I notice there are cars coming and parking. And people—people children and adult people—are getting out of the cars and going inside the school, just as though it's morning when school starts instead of afternoon when it's over.

I ask myself: *Did I fall asleep in the afternoon and miss the night and now it's morning?*

Squirrels don't usually get confused that way.

Besides, if this was morning, I decide, I'd be hungrier.

But no, this *is* afternoon, and yet people are going *into* the school.

Why?

I am within a mystery story of my own, I realize.

I must go into the school and investigate.

Sweetie:
The Library Rat

I love living in the school's library even though my friend Twitch the squirrel shudders at the idea of being a pet and living in a cage.

I tell him, "I never have to look for food. Miss Krause the librarian always makes sure I have enough." Twitch needs to gather his own food, and then he has to hide it so none of the other animals who live outside can get to it before he does. Sometimes he forgets where he's hidden whatever he's gathered, and he has to start all over again.

I tell him, "I don't need to worry about cold weather,

or wet weather, or animals that eat rats." Sometimes I see Twitch through the window in the library, and he looks cold or wet. Or sometimes he's there hiding from something that's big and hungry and fierce.

I tell him, "This is a library, so Miss Krause is always reading stories to the students." Twitch loves stories almost as much as I do, but he tells me he doesn't need to hear the exact words that are in the books, and that I tell them fine enough. He says he doesn't need to hear the funny voices Miss Krause uses, and he doesn't need to see the pictures. But sometimes I see him pressing his ear to the window when Miss Krause is reading to the children. Sometimes he stands on tiptoes on the ledge to see the pictures.

Today I'm sad to be living in a cage in the library, because there's something going on in another part of the school where I have never been. It is something I'd very much like to see, but I will only hear about it tomorrow after it's all over.

Miss Krause has written a play, which the children will be performing in the auditorium for their parents. Miss Krause wrote the words, and Mr. Ziegler, the music teacher, wrote songs, both of them making sure there would be parts for all the children who wanted to be in the play. Over the past few weeks, I have sometimes heard the children practicing. (Practicing for a play is called *rehearsing*.) I have learned all about plays, and acting, and how a stage is set up, even though I have only seen drawings of a stage, not the actual stage that is in the school auditorium.

I would so much love to see the play. The story is my absolute favorite: *Cinderella*. There are many fine things about the story of Cinderella, but the best part is that the hero is a rat. It is the rat who drives the coach that gets Cinderella to the ball so that she can meet the prince after her cruel stepmother and stepsisters have forbidden her to go.

Very often people write stories where rats are the bad guys. But Cinderella's rat coachman is a good role model for anyone.

Of course there will not be a real rat in the play, but a boy dressed up like a rat. The boy who will play the part of the rat is named Liam. When Liam checks out books from the library, they are always ones that tell how things are made, or how they work. He has been practicing being a rat by sitting in front of my cage and watching me. When I scratch my ear, he scratches his ear. The first time he did this, he sat on the floor and bent his leg to get his foot close to his head. Miss Krause told him to use his front paw. So now he uses his hands to scratch his ear as well as to pretend to wash his pretend whiskers. (Mr. Ziegler has whiskers, but Liam does not.)

Still, I wish I could see it. But I will have to satisfy myself with hearing about it. Tomorrow.

Twitch:
A Play

Someone has placed a block of wood to keep the school door from locking behind each person that goes in. Not counting in the morning when the people children normally arrive, if you want to get into the school, you need to push the little button by the door and tell who you are.

This is very inconvenient for squirrels.

That's why, if I want to get in, I usually look for an open window. It doesn't need to be open all that much because I am very good at squeezing through a small space.

But today, because of the block of wood, I don't need to find a window. I just wait until nobody is looking, then I dash into the school. I have to be a little bit sneaky, because people love squirrels so much there is always the risk that someone will try to catch me and keep me as a pet.

Inside, I see the people who I watched going in before me. They are standing in front of a long table where some other people are sitting and talking to them. The just-coming-in people and the sitting-there people trade pieces of paper back and forth.

Nobody sees me even though I run right by them.

People aren't very good at keeping a careful lookout. They're lucky they're so big, or owls and foxes would always be swooping in and carrying them off to snack on them.

I run down the hall to the room called *library*. I have a cousin who lives there.

He is a rat, and his name is Sweetie. Sweetie is much smarter than most of my other cousins, including some of my squirrel cousins. This is true even though he chooses to live in a cage in the school. Sweetie is smart enough that he can open the cage, so he could escape if he wanted to. But he likes the people, and he likes the treats they give him—especially the yogurt drops—and most of all he likes the people stories he hears in the library.

I like the yogurt drops, too—Sweetie shares them with me if he has any left over when I come to visit. And I like the stories. But I'm willing to wait and hear them after the people are gone.

In the library, I scramble up the leg of a chair, to be able to jump up onto the table, and then I run the length of the table and leap to the bookcase where Sweetie's cage sits.

I think the *thump!* of my landing wakes him up—rats are more active during the night, so he takes a lot of naps during the day—but he doesn't complain. He just stretches and yawns and says, "Hello, Twitch. I'm happy to see you. Have you come for a story?"

"I have," I tell him. "But meanwhile, I was wondering: why are people coming back to school in the afternoon?"

Sweetie opens the cage door, but I don't go in. I feel safe and happy *outside* the cage. Sweetie feels safe and happy *inside* the cage. But the open door is friendlier than talking through the bars. So, with Sweetie inside and me outside, Sweetie starts grooming his tail, and he tells me, "It's the play."

I ask, "They've come back to play?" Usually the people children play outside, at least during the good weather. And usually the people parents don't stay. I think: *Maybe the children and their parents will all play together inside.*

But Sweetie says, "*Play* as a noun, not a verb."

I say, "What?" Sweetie is sometimes too smart. That comes from living in a school rather than in a schoolyard.

He says, "A play is a story that is acted out."

I say, "I have heard some of the people children get scolded for acting out, but I'm not really sure what *acting out* means."

Sweetie scratches his ear. "Let's start over. Sometimes I tell you a story . . ."

I say, "And sometimes *I* tell *you* a story. Have I told you this one? Once I found a whole bunch of acorns and I buried them, but then I couldn't remember where I'd put them. But then I found them again."

"Yes, you *have* told me that story," Sweetie says. "And it's a very good one. But in a play, instead of just telling the words, you would show the actions. Like this." Sweetie runs from one end of his cage to the other. He uses a bigger-than-normal voice and asks, "Oh dear, oh dear, where have I put my acorns?"

I say, "You've lost acorns, too?"

Sweetie shakes his head but keeps looking, digging beneath the shredded paper that covers the floor of his cage. He says, "I know I buried them here someplace."

I say, "Maybe they're in that corner by your food dish."

Sweetie shakes his head again so that I wonder if he has a flea in his ear. Then he runs to where I'm pointing and digs up a yogurt drop he's put there for safekeeping. "Here's my acorn!" he says. "Yay! I found it."

"Sweetie," I tell him, "that's not an acorn. That's a yogurt drop."

Sweetie sighs. Going back to his normal voice, he says,

"I know. I was acting out your story. I was pretending to be you. That's what a play is."

"Oh," I say. He didn't sound like me at all. But I tell him, "I see. Are you going to eat that yogurt drop?"

Sweetie hands me the yogurt drop, because he's a good friend. He says, "So the children are putting on a play, and their parents have come to watch."

"A play about me and my acorns?" I ask. People love squirrels, so naturally they'd want to watch a play about me. I just don't know how they knew my story to make a play out of it.

"No," Sweetie tells me. "It's the story of Cinderella."

I stop chewing the yogurt drop while I consider. Do I know this story?

Sweetie says, "It's about a rat who becomes a coachman and helps this girl, Cinderella, get to the ball so she can meet the prince so that the two of them can live happily ever after. It's my favorite."

This sounds vaguely familiar, but I can't remember all the details. I ask, "Cinderella and the rat live happily ever after? Or the prince and the rat? Does the rat play with the ball? Is it one of those really bouncy balls or is it the kind that people toss back and forth to each other?"

Sweetie looks confused, so maybe he can't remember all the details, either. "None of the above," he tells me.

"Okay," I say. "Will they play the play here in the library?"

"No." Sweetie's tail droops. "They'll put on the play at a special place they call a stage." Has there ever been a sadder-looking rat? When Sweetie was acting out my story about looking for the acorns, he made his voice bigger than normal. Now his voice is smaller than normal when he tells me, "It's a long way from the library to the auditorium where the stage is."

"But Cinderella is your favorite story," I point out.

He sighs. A rat sighing is a very sorrowful sound. "I'll hear them talk about it tomorrow."

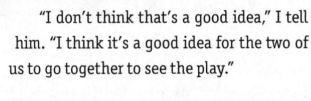

"I don't think that's a good idea," I tell him. "I think it's a good idea for the two of us to go together to see the play."

Sweetie:
The Quest

I say to Twitch, "I'd love to see the play, but I'm too likely to get lost on my way to the auditorium."

Twitch shakes his head. "You can have an adventure, like in an adventure story. People in adventure stories get lost all the time. But then they find their way. And then they live happily ever after."

"That would be nice," I say. "But I can't see well enough to find my way. Albino rats like me—rats with white fur and red eyes—we can't see as well as rats with dark fur and dark eyes."

"You have red eyes?" he asks.

He leans close and peers into my eyes. "You do!" he tells me. "You *do* have red eyes."

"I know," I tell him.

"But you can see me," he points out. "And you can see well enough to open the cage. And sometimes you leave."

I can. But I don't often. Usually I just sit on the bookcase with Twitch, sharing stories and munching yogurt drops.

I explain, "I can see things that are close up. That's why, when I leave the cage, I like to stay close to something. I'm not so good with crossing open spaces."

Twitch's expression tells me he may well never have noticed this. Still, he says, "But I can go with you. I can guide you. We can go on an adventure together."

This might work! I stand tall and happy. "You could be like my Seeing Eye dog," I say.

"Sweetie"—Twitch moves in closer so I can see him better—"it's me: Twitch the squirrel—not a dog."

"I know that," I say.

"I'm glad we have that cleared up," he says.

I tell him, "It will be a quest for the two of us."

"Right," he says, but he sounds a bit unsure.

I explain, "A quest is when the heroes of the story are looking for something."

"Like acorns!" he exclaims. "My favorite!"

"Usually something bigger," I say.

"Like walnuts!" he exclaims. "My favorite!"

I step out of my cage and walk to the edge of the bookcase. I climb down while Twitch hovers anxiously, concerned now that he knows I can't see very well.

Once I'm down, he jumps from the bookcase to the table to the chair to the floor. "It's me," he announces, moving in close and waving his arms, just in case I can't see him.

"I know," I assure him.

"So how do we get to where the people children will be playing their play?" he asks. But a moment later he catches on. "Right," he says. "If you knew, you could have gone on your own."

I say, "But in any case, it's more fun to go on a quest with a friend. We can follow the parents who are coming into the school. But they can't see us."

"Are they albinos with white fur and red eyes who can't see well?" he asks.

"No," I explain, "I meant to say we can't *let them* see us."

Twitch nods. "Because we are so cute they would want to make us into pets," he agrees.

I don't point out that I already am a pet.

We walk to the door of the library. Twitch gets there in four bounds. I go more slowly, taking little steps and following the wall.

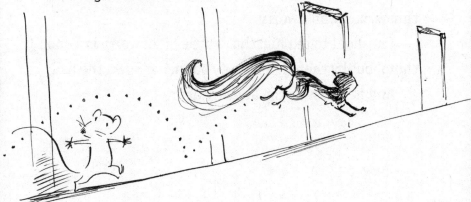

Twitch peeks out the door and looks both ways. "No people here," he says. "The people I saw coming in were around that corner there." He's facing the direction of the main hall. And in another moment he's gone. He runs to the corner and looks, then runs back to where I'm waiting. He tells me, "A bunch of people are in the hall by the door they used to get into the school. But they're not going back outside. They're going through another door."

That must be the auditorium, where the stage is. "Okay," I say, "we'll take it one doorway at a time."

Clearly Twitch is worried this will take a long while. Squirrels always bound and leap and run, always in a hurry. He asks, "What if the play is over by the time we get there?"

"Don't worry. They won't start until the people in the hallway have all gone in."

Twitch tells me, "You're very smart and know these things, so I won't worry."

I'm about to tell him that a little bit of worry is a good thing, but by then he's already bouncing down the hall.

And he doesn't stop at every door.

Twitch:
The Audy-Toy-Room

I dash and bounce down the first hallway, then around the corner toward the door where the people are clustered like pigeons after someone has thrown down bread crumbs for a squirrel and the pigeons think the bread is for them.

When I'm almost at the door where the play will be played, I turn to ask Sweetie right there behind me, *Isn't this fun?*

Except Sweetie isn't right there behind me.

Or even far back behind me.

I check both walls and finally spot him *way* back, peeking his head around the corner of the hall where the library is. He hasn't gotten far at all.

He waves his tiny pink paw at me.

I wave back.

He waves a second time, and I realize he isn't so much *waving* as gesturing *come back*.

I dash and bounce back to where he is waiting.

"We don't want the people to see us," he tells me.

"Of course not," I agree.

We stay where we are, just outside the library, peeking out and waiting until everybody has gone through the doors into what Sweetie calls the audy-toy-room, which is where the people have assemblies (whatever *they* are) and plays (which I've just learned everything there is to know about).

Finally, everyone has gone in, except for the children who have been handing everyone sheets of paper.

Sweetie is nervous about showing ourselves while the way is mostly, but not totally, clear. But he also says we must hurry because the doors will be closed soon and that will make it difficult for us to get in to watch the play.

Once more I dash and bounce down the hall, trying to remember to stay close to the wall and to hide for a moment in each doorway—well, most doorways . . . well, some doorways—to check to make sure no one is looking our way, which Sweetie has asked me to do.

I get to the doors just as the two handing-out-papers children are closing them.

"What was that?" I hear one of them ask as I take the quickest route, which is over his foot.

The lights are dim in the audy-toy-room, and the second child asks, "What was what?"

Luckily, this gives Sweetie the chance to catch up because I forgot to wait for him, and he doesn't so much dash and bounce as scurry and scamper. But now we're both in, and the children haven't seen us, and they close the doors. Without the light from the hall, the audy-toy-room seems dark, but squirrels have excellent vision in the dark.

Still, I don't see any toys in this audy-toy-room.

What I see is that we are in back of rows and rows of chairs all facing a wall. The people are sitting looking at the wall, and nobody is talking.

I don't know exactly what Sweetie can see, but he

scurries under the nearest chair and motions for me to join him quickly. "Out of the aisle," he tells me.

I balance on my back legs to look around, and I ask, "What's an aisle?"

He doesn't answer but only motions again, and I go under the chair.

Except it isn't a chair. There's a back, but no seat. Is everyone in this room not actually *sitting* but *balancing* on seatless chairs? Are these chairs the toys?

In another moment the children who were at the door move to where we are. They pull down the seats, which were there all along, just somehow up against the backs. They sit down in the chair Sweetie and I are crouched under and the one next to it. Luckily, we are far enough back that they don't step on us.

"Now what?" I ask Sweetie, but before I even finish asking, music starts playing, and the people clap. I have heard children play music before. Their teacher doesn't usually clap. He usually says, "Someone has not been practicing." I don't know if he means himself or the child, or if by *someone* he means somebody else entirely. You'd think a teacher would be clearer about something like that.

Sweetie leans out from the side of the chair we're under and into the path that he called *the aisle*. "That's the stage," he tells me, pointing in the direction all the people have been facing. "Where the play is acted out."

I, too, peek out from under the chair, and I see that the wall way up in front is rising into the ceiling. Most walls don't do that. Lights from all over the audy-toy-room are pointing there, showing there is a whole other room that we can only see now because that one wall went up. In that room, a bunch of the people children start to walk around and sing.

Sweetie: Cinderella!

In the auditorium, Twitch and I are sitting under the chairs of the children who were handing out the programs that tell about the play and the actors. I know all the children who come to the library. The girl is Delaney, and she likes spooky books, and the boy is Cyrus, who likes poetry.

The lights dim, which means people are less likely to see us.

The orchestra starts playing, which means people are less likely to hear us.

And the curtain goes up, which means the play is beginning.

But closer to me I hear a crinkly sound that I recognize. Delaney is opening a food wrapper.

Twitch says, "I haven't eaten since you shared your yogurt drop with me forever ago," and I hear his tummy rumble.

My own tummy lets me know now might be a nice time for a snack.

I sniff but can't smell what food is being unwrapped.

Twitch's nose expectantly tests the air, too.

"What do they have?" he asks me.

"Hard to say," I whisper. "I don't think she's gotten the bag open yet."

The chair above us moves a bit as Delaney struggles with the bag.

Twitch's jaw moves and he clenches a paw. I know him well enough to know he is thinking that teeth and claws are more useful than fingers, and that *he* could get the bag open. I put my small, bare paw on his bigger, furry one, and I shake my head to let him know he shouldn't offer to help her.

One more jerk of the chair, and we hear Delaney whisper, "Oops!" just as we get the whiff of salt and butter and—

"Popcorn!" Twitch says. "My favorite food ever!" As

several pieces rain down on our heads, he tells me, "How kind of the girl to share!"

Twitch and I grab up the pieces from the floor. Delicious!

Around the popcorn in his mouth, Twitch tells me, "I love this play!"

I tell him, "The food isn't part of the play."

"Oh yes it is!" he answers. "The food is a very tasty part of the play."

I consider. "Well, it's part of the play, but the play is more about what is said and done onstage."

"Nobody is saying anything," Twitch complains. "They can't. Those people children won't stop singing."

"That's part of the play," I tell him. "Listen to the words. Those are townspeople, and they're saying through their song how sad it is that Cinderella's mother died. Then her father found someone else who was supposed to be a mother to Cinderella. Her name is Stepmother, because she's one step away from being Cinderella's mother. But Stepmother already had two daughters, called the stepsisters, and they were mean to Cinderella. Then the father died, and then Stepmother started to be mean to Cinderella, too, and now Stepmother and the stepsisters force her to do all the work and to sleep by the fireplace."

"Wow, we missed a lot of the play while we were enjoying that popcorn," Twitch says.

"No," I explain, "they're talking about things that already happened before the play began."

"Okay," Twitch says doubtfully. But then he says, "Oh, like in my story, the one about finding acorns, then burying them, then not being able to remember where I buried them, and then finally finding them again. When you were acting my story out, you didn't include the parts about finding the acorns or burying them. You just started by running around in your cage and asking, 'Where have I put my acorns?' So this is like that."

Sometimes following what Twitch is saying can make me dizzy. "Yes," I say once I've worked it out.

I'm watching the play, but we're too far away for me to be able to make out the faces of the children I know. We're so far away, I can't make out that there *are* children on the stage. Just blob shapes. Moving. And singing.

"Can you see?" Twitch asks.

"I can hear," I say. "That's good enough."

"No." His voice is forceful. "It's *not* good enough. Let's move closer."

"We have to be careful," I warn him.

"Of course," he tells me. "We'll be so careful no one will even know we're here."

I'm thinking: _Can Twitch be that careful?_

But he's already dashed away.

Twitch:
The Cinderella Play

Of course I'm worried about Sweetie. I want him to be able to see the play.

But I'm also thinking that the girl and the boy in the seats above us haven't dropped any popcorn in a while. Maybe there *is* no more popcorn in their bag. Maybe somebody closer to the stage will have some different food.

We start moving, keeping under the chairs, as we make for what he calls *the stage,* which is downhill from where we started.

There isn't any more popcorn on the floor, but there *is* a piece of gum. It's been there for a while, so it's gotten stepped on, but I can still smell some flavor on it. I'm not sure *what* the flavor is, but it smells delicious. I stop moving forward and pick at the gum. It's really stuck. I pull harder and some of it comes up, in a long sticky string that's still attached to the floor. I pull harder. *Thwack!* The string snaps, and the end of the gum smacks me between the eyes.

And sticks there.

I pull the gum, but it just stretches. And meanwhile I lose my balance—just a little bit—and I brush against the ankle of the person sitting in the seat above me. The man yelps as though I've bitten him. I haven't. But that's what he sounds like.

The woman next to him whispers, "What is it, dear?"

The man has the paper those children handed him when he came in, and he swats at his ankle. I've moved away, so he can't see me, but that doesn't stop him from swatting away.

I remain motionless like a tree root, which is good squirrel strategy if you are upwind from a fox, or if you're not wanting to be seen while you're under a chair in an audy-toy-room, clutching one end of a piece of gum while the other end is stuck to your face.

"Something's there," the man tells the woman, not exactly out loud, but not as quiet as she was. "Do you have your phone handy?"

She leans down to look, and she has one of those things that people have that can shine a light, but Sweetie and I have moved to beneath the seat in front of the one in front of them, with another set of feet between us and them, and she doesn't shine the light that far; she's only shining it at his feet. "I don't see anything," she tells him.

"Shh," other people tell the two of them.

"Be careful," Sweetie tells me as we start moving again.

"I *am*," I tell him. My tail flicks in annoyance at his unnecessary instruction, and the person whose chair we're passing under gives a shrill *"Whoop!"*

The gum I have scraped up from the floor is sticky as I continue to try to pick it off my face, and now it's stuck to my paws, too. Meanwhile my tail might—maybe—brush against another ankle. The foot attached to the ankle kicks out. I know this is accidental. I know that the person I might have maybe brushed against doesn't know he's kicked a squirrel—because everyone loves squirrels.

And I'm not hurt. But I go rolling on the slick floor—downhill, toward the stage, the string of gum wrapping itself around me. My tail flips this way and that as I try to regain stability.

There are more *whoops!* as well as *yips!* and *yikes!* from the people whose chairs I've slid beneath. More feet are lashing out, and I'm trying to avoid them before I've quite caught my balance, all the while staggering forward.

Behind me, I hear Sweetie panting as he tries to keep up so that he doesn't lose me, and he's saying things like "Oops!" and "Sorry!" and "Beg pardon!" because he's a polite rat, even though people can't understand him. They probably hear his squeaks. I'm guessing this by their squeals and by the sound of chair seats going *sproing!*

smack! as they flip back up because the people in them have jumped to their feet.

People in the back loudly whisper, "Down in front!"

I suddenly find that there is no chair above me. I have ended up in the space between the chairs where the parents are sitting and other chairs where the children who are making music are sitting.

A girl who is blowing into a silver tube sees me. Her eyes get big, and the tube makes a *skritch!* noise. Mr. Ziegler, the music teacher, has *not* seen me. He has his back to me as he stands directing the music, just as he does in class. Except in class he would have stopped everybody and told the girl to try again, and now he just gives a slight shudder as though the *skritch!* hurt his ears. He looks over his shoulder to glare at the parents fussing and not paying attention. *Paying attention* is an important rule in his class. With his hand he motions for the girl to continue playing. By now, I've backed under the chair, and the girl once more puts the tube to her mouth.

I work at picking gum off my tail, but by now I've lost interest in eating it as it has bits of my fur all over it. I spit pieces of furry gum onto the floor.

I'm almost pushed out from under the chair as Sweetie runs into my back end.

"Sorry! Sorry!" he says. But he sounds more relieved to have found me than sorry that he's run into me.

"Well," I tell him, "now we're closer. But now we can't see the play at all, because the children making music are in the way."

Even sitting, they're too tall to see over, at least from where we are, down here at the bottom of the hill in the audy-toy-room.

"That's fine," Sweetie assures me. "We can listen."

I can see that the stage is up higher than the rest of the floor. Probably the people sitting on the chairs uphill can see what's going on much better than the squirrel and the rat sitting *underneath* the chairs.

But from here I can see something I didn't notice before. There are three steps. Squirrels can count to three, because three is an important number: Mother, Father, me. You, me, other. Good to eat, better to eat, best to eat. So I can count to three, and I see there are three steps leading from the floor where we are—one, two, three—up to the stage where the play is being played.

I tell Sweetie, "I have a plan."

Sweetie:
Backstage

One of the things I admire about Twitch is his fearlessness, the way he will throw himself into anything.

I admire that, but I don't want to be like that.

I can see where he is looking, and I can guess what his plan is. *I* do not want to go up the steps leading to the stage. "No, no, no, no, no!" I squeak. "This is not a good plan!"

"Of course it is!" he tells me. "Would I come up with a bad plan? Now run!"

He runs past the children playing in the orchestra and bounds up the stairs.

I do not want to be left behind, so I follow as fast as my shorter legs will carry me. Even though the last thing we should do is call attention to ourselves, I cannot help myself. I cannot help squeaking, "No! No! No! No! No!" all the way to the stairs and onto the stage.

On each side there are curtains that never move because they're there to block the audience from seeing into the wings, where actors wait to perform and where crew members wait to help move furniture or hand out props.

I call to Twitch, "Behind the curtain!"

"What's a curtain?" he asks, but this time *he* follows *me*. We duck behind the curtain. Now the audience can't see us; and the orchestra and Mr. Ziegler, who is conducting, can't see us. But we can see the children who are playing the townspeople, singing about poor Cinderella.

I am at the play! Close up enough to mostly be able to see. I'm as excited as Cinderella will be once she gets to go to the ball.

Twitch is looking all around, and I explain to him that we are *backstage* and that people probably won't notice us here if we are careful.

Twitch flicks his tail, which still has bits of gum in it. "I'm always careful," he assures me.

The townspeople finish their song and leave. They were on the part of the stage called the apron—just the very front part—and now the second curtain opens in the middle to reveal the rest of the stage, which is the set for the home of Cinderella and her family.

One of the stepsisters sings:

"Cinderella, sweep the floor.
Cinderella, get the door.
Work all day and into the night:
watching you work is my delight."

The second stepsister sings:

"Cinderella, fetch my pearls.
Cinderella, brush my curls.
Work all day and into the night:
making you work is my delight."

The stepmother sings:

"Cinderella, stir my tea.
Cinderella, sew for me.
Work all day and into the night:
you serving me is my delight."

Every once in a while all three sing together:

"Cinderella, Cinderella, do each chore.
And when you're done, you can do some more."

Meanwhile, they take turns pushing Cinderella around.

I know these girls. The stepmother is Sophie, who helps out in the library and likes nonfiction books, especially those about cute baby animals. The stepsisters are real-life sisters, Jazaniya and J'Honesty, and they both like chapter books. Even though they are best friends with Ainsley, the girl who is playing Cinderella (who likes stories set in different lands), they are good actors, and they make themselves look and sound mean.

"Can you see?" I ask Twitch. I am *so* pleased to be where I can hear *and* see.

"I don't know if I like this play," he tells me. "The teachers shouldn't let those children treat that girl that way. It makes me want to bite them."

"No!" I squeak. "No biting. Never, never biting in school. And that girl is Cinderella, and she will be happy by the time the play ends, after the rat helps her get to the ball so she can meet the prince."

Twitch must guess I'm right, since he knows I know the story, but he clearly doesn't like to watch all this meanness. Instead, he looks around where we are.

I should probably worry about that.

I *know* I should worry about it.

Instead, I watch the play.

Twitch:
Walls That Move

I turn away from the three girls who are being mean to the plus-one girl.

The girls who were onstage being townspeople have taken off the scarves that they were wearing draped over their heads or shoulders or around their waists, and now they toss them into a pile on the floor. From a metal rack like the ones in classrooms for hanging up outside clothes, the girls choose long, sparkly skirts in bright colors, which they put on over the plain skirts they were wearing already—which makes the new ones poof out. The girls twirl to make the skirts poof out even more. In between twirling, they put beads around their necks and wrists.

The townspeople boys toss the hats they were wearing onto the floor with the girls' scarves and they choose tight-fitting jackets with rows of bright buttons. There are strips of shiny something-or-other that they stick to the sides of their legs to give their pants fancy stripes. The boys are having a good time putting the strips on, then peeling them off, which makes an I-don't-want-to-let-go noise that catches the attention of one of the teachers who is watching from backstage.

She scolds boys and girls alike in a sharp whisper. "Stop that before the audience hears you."

"Yes, Miss Krause," they say. "Sorry, Miss Krause."

This is the teacher in the library, where Sweetie lives. She looks friendlier when she's in the library. Now she looks as though she doesn't believe the *sorries* and suspects the children are ready to misbehave as soon as she leaves. So she continues to stand there, glaring at them.

I know from past experience that nothing interesting happens while a teacher is glaring at children. I've gotten bored with picking gum out of my fur, so I let my attention wander to the cloth walls that Sweetie called curtains, and I wonder: *Do all the curtains go up? And where do they go up to?* Sweetie is too busy watching the play to answer questions, so I will quietly investigate.

I climb up the curtain Sweetie and I are standing behind, the one off to the side. Squirrels are excellent climbers. We are used to climbing trees, so we are not afraid of heights.

The three mean people stop singing and leave the stage, walking right by Sweetie without seeing him, and right under me without seeing me.

The Cinderella girl sings by herself—that she wishes she could go somewhere else, somewhere where she could love someone and be loved in return.

Her song reminds me of the sad stories moles tell.

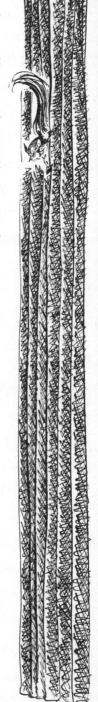

Then, all of a sudden, my cloth wall starts to move. It doesn't go up, the way the first curtain did. It moves sideways. The curtain from the other side of the stage moves also, until my curtain and the other curtain meet in the middle. I continue to hang on—squirrels are very good at hanging on—and I wait to see what will happen next.

Now that the people in the audy-toy-room can't see them, the children on the backstage side of the curtain start moving furniture, taking away the tables and chairs that were part of Cinderella's home and moving other pieces of furniture onto the stage to replace them.

Meanwhile, the play continues on the other side of the wall made of curtain I'm hanging on to. I hear children talking. One is called King, one is called Queen, and one is called Prince.

I can hear them, but I can't see them.

So I climb sideways, to where the two pieces of cloth wall meet, and I peek my head out and watch.

King and Queen say they want to have a ball. Sweetie mentioned a ball, but I can't remember what he said about it. Prince says he does not want a ball. This surprises me because most children like to play with balls. Sometimes they throw them at each other, or sometimes they bounce them off a wall. Maybe Prince does not want the ball because the walls here are all cloth, so a ball wouldn't bounce properly.

The parents who are watching the play are not paying attention to King, Queen, and Prince. Some of them have started whispering among themselves. Teachers normally do not permit that kind of behavior. Some of the parents are giggling. Some are pointing at the stage.

Oops, wait, no: they're pointing at me.

I pull my head out from between the curtains, but now I see that the people backstage have seen me, too. Miss Krause has the stick-thing Cinderella was using to sweep the floor. I think she plans to sweep me down so that she can put me in a cage and keep me as a pet along with Sweetie.

Once more I poke my head to the other side to check who is nearer to me, Miss Krause or King and Queen and Prince.

They are not near at all. They have jumped off the stage and are covering their heads—as though afraid I might fall off the curtain and onto them. Clearly, they don't know squirrels.

I flip over to their side of the curtain, even though now even the least-alert parent people can see me. But I can move fast. I skid and slide down the curtain to the floor and run to the other side of the stage to get away from Miss Krause.

I run backstage on this new side, then I scramble underneath the cloth wall that is in back. There is *more* backstage. It must be *back* backstage. There are great big pieces of cardboard with paintings of trees, or building fronts, or walls, and I hide between two of them. I hear Miss Krause saying in a loud whisper, "Find that creature!" But I am an excellent hider.

Even hiding, I hear some of the parents from the audy-toy-room laughing and clapping for me, calling out, "Go, Squirrel!"

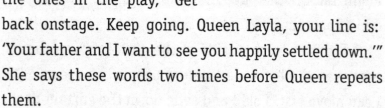

That's because everyone loves squirrels.

Meanwhile, Miss Krause is urging the other children, the ones in the play, "Get back onstage. Keep going. Queen Layla, your line is: 'Your father and I want to see you happily settled down.'" She says these words two times before Queen repeats them.

I wait until the children onstage are once more talking about the ball, and the children searching for me have given up.

I cross over the *back* backstage, then scootch under the cloth wall to where I left Sweetie when he and I were standing watching the play.

He isn't there.

Sweetie:
Listening for Twitch

As soon as the people in the audience start murmuring and giggling, my fur stands on end, the same as it does when a new parent meets me for the first time and says, "A rat? Really? A rat is not an appropriate pet for a school library." (Miss Krause always speaks up on my behalf, and in the end her words persuade the parents that I am totally appropriate—her words *and* my doing everything anybody has ever declared to be cute. But this feels like that first moment when I worry that Miss Krause won't be able to convince them and that disaster might follow.)

Is disaster about to follow *this* moment?

I look to my left, and to my right, and behind me, even though I already know what I'll see—or rather, what I won't see. Sure enough, Twitch is no longer standing near me. I can't see him, but I can see that people—both backstage and in the audience—have their heads tipped back. They are looking high up at the curtain that is supposed to be a castle hallway. The parents are pointing, and now they are laughing out loud.

Twitch is too far away for me to be able to see him, but I don't need to see him to know that somehow he has come to be hanging from the curtain.

The king, the queen, and the prince have been acting out a scene. (The king is played by Eduardo, who prefers to read sports magazines rather than books, though lately Miss Krause has introduced him to storybooks that include people playing sports. The queen is played by Layla, whose favorites are biographies about girls who grow into strong women. And the prince is played by Victor, who likes books that have anything to do with science.)

Now all three have jumped off the stage. I have watched the children practicing in the library, and I don't remember any part of the play where the actors are directed to jump off the stage and say their lines from the auditorium floor. The children try to continue, but Victor repeats something he's already said, and Layla blurts out something that isn't supposed to come until the scene at the ball. Eduardo says, "Tut! Tut! It might be time to call in the Court Pest Control Squad." This doesn't make any sense, since Twitch is a squirrel, not a pest.

The royal family gives up on saying their lines, and they turn and stare at the curtain along with everyone else.

If he was here, I would ask Twitch: *Is this being careful?*

But if he was here, I wouldn't have to ask him because none of this would be happening.

The children who are backstage crowd closer to get a better look. I jump to the side, just in time to avoid a sixth-grade boy's big feet. I better find someplace to hide where I won't get stepped on.

While I'm looking around for where that might be, I notice Miss Krause sending some of the children to look for Twitch. I tell myself not to worry about him: he is very

good at being a squirrel and that means avoiding getting caught by owls, dogs, foxes, or children.

I see a big pile of cast-off costumes that the children used when they were being townspeople. They won't need these again and won't bother hanging them up till the play is over, so I'll be safe burrowing into the heap of clothing.

Even though that means I won't be able to see the play.

But I settle in and listen as the audience settles down, and the actors once more start reciting their lines and singing their songs.

It's nice and cozy in here, with the pieces of material carrying the smell of some of my favorite library people.

I think I'll rest my eyes, just for a bit . . .

Twitch:
Where's Sweetie?

Oh, no! Where's Sweetie?

Did one of the people find him and take him back to his cage in the library? Will he be in trouble? (This is something the children often worry about, warning each other: "Ooo, you're in trouble now.") What if Miss Krause finds a way to lock his cage so that he can't get out anymore?

This couldn't be my fault, could it?

But while I'm thinking all this, I'm noticing the play is still being played on what Sweetie called the stage. The Cinderella girl is being bossed around—even more than before—by the other three people. Someone has told them about the ball, and unlike the prince, *they* are all excited about it.

The stepmother girl orders Cinderella: "Fetch our best gowns from the chests."

One of the stepsister girls orders Cinderella: "Brush my hair."

The second stepsister girl orders Cinderella: "But first, draw a bath for me."

I have seen children draw things before. Sometimes I have trouble telling what it is they've drawn. Sometimes the teachers have trouble telling what it is they've drawn. I don't know what a bath is, but I don't have time to watch the Cinderella girl draw one.

I turn away, but I hear Stepmother tell the two other girls to stop arguing. "There's more than enough time to prepare," she tells them. "Be calm, my sweets."

Uh-oh! *Sweets* reminds me: I'm supposed to be looking for Sweetie.

Backstage, Miss Krause seems to be in charge—not only of finding squirrels but of everything. She tells this child, "Go here," she tells that child, "Go there," she tells them all, "No talking," even though she's talking.

Now I hear her ask, "Where are the musicians for the ball scene?"

"Here," says a boy pushing a smaller version of the piano the music teacher sometimes thumps on.

"Here," says a boy holding a tube like the one held by the girl who saw me before I ran up the stairs and onto the stage.

"Here," says another child. "But one of the strings on my lute broke."

"That's all right," Miss Krause says. "No one from the audience will know."

She seems to be too busy to worry about me. Good.

I stay close to the cloth walls so that I can always run under them if I need to hide in a hurry. I look for Sweetie. "Sweetie! Sweetie!" I call. Maybe I should return to the library in case he's there. But what if he isn't *there*—what if he's *here*? What if he needs me and I'm back in the library?

Stay or go? So many decisions!

Why oh why did I ever leave him on his own?

"Sweetie!" I call louder than before. It's Sweetie's eyes that are weak, not his ears. But it seems that—wherever he is—Sweetie can't see or hear me.

From the pile of clothes the children have shed onto the floor, I catch a faint whiff of Sweetie. I run over and start pawing through the hats and scarves.

There's a squeak, but it's not from within the pile, and it's not from Sweetie.

It's Miss Krause, looking directly at me, trying to hold me with her gaze. "Marc," she says to one of the boys, "get something to capture him in."

Capture? As in . . . *capture*?

"What should I get?" the Marc boy asks.

"That library bin we used to carry the props," Miss Krause says. "Quickly. But quietly."

I knew it! She wants to have me as a library pet.
I dive off the pile of clothing to make my escape.
But a scarf is caught on one of my toenails.
I make a quick circle, trying to shake it loose.

And another scarf attaches itself to me, clinging to the gum that's still stuck on my tail. (I knew I should have worked on that!)

Still, I run, trailing the two scarves.

I dodge around Miss Krause, making sure I stay far enough away that she won't be able to grab me—

—and she puts her foot down on the scarf stuck to my tail. The scarf tugs.

But then comes free.

A tuft of my tail fur comes free with it.

Ouch!

But I don't stop.

Some of the other children from backstage have begun to gather, blocking the way to *back* backstage, and I don't want any of them to step on the toenail scarf in case that would pull my toenail free.

So I run around the curtain and onto the stage where the three-plus-one—one stepmother, two stepsisters, and Cinderella—are still singing about getting ready for the ball.

"Eeek!" cries Stepmother, jumping off the stage. She lands so close to the music teacher that he drops the stick he uses for leading the music.

"Eeek!" cries Stepsister One. She also jumps off the stage, and she knocks down one of the music stands.

"Eeek!" cries Stepsister Two. She claws at where the two sides of the curtain meet and runs backstage. I can't see where she goes, but she knocks into something-or-other back there, which lands with a clatter.

The plus-one, Cinderella, doesn't cry *"Eeek!"* And she doesn't jump or run anywhere. She just steps aside to let me pass.

I leap onto the curtain behind her. From a safe

distance up, I'm able to take the time to chew at the scarf till it comes loose from my toenail and drifts down to the floor.

The parents cheer and clap.

Cinderella picks up the scarf and fastens it across her shoulders as though that was exactly what she was waiting for. "Yes, Stepmother," she calls down to Stepmother, still standing among the music players. "I will get everything ready for you." Then, twirling the end of her scarf, she walks off to the side backstage.

I run across the curtain in the opposite direction, where I jump off and run around back to once more hide among the cardboard trees and walls.

Still without Sweetie.

Sweetie:
Hiding

Twitch's voice reaches into my dream of rolling around in sunflower seeds and wakes me up. What a time to take a nap—during the play! And with Twitch running all over the stage! But I *have* been very busy, what with escaping from the library, dashing down hallways, running under auditorium seats, and worrying, worrying, worrying. This might not seem like much to a rat in the wild, but for a library rat, it's about a day and a half's worth of activity in one short afternoon.

I claw through all the scarves and shawls until I'm

finally able to poke my nose up from the depths of the pile of already-used costumes.

Right away, I poke my nose back under a hat. Twitch is here, but so is Miss Krause—and she's looking right at him! In another moment, Twitch leaps away, and Miss Krause takes off after him.

Did she see me? I don't think so, but I can't be sure. Miss Krause likes me, but she won't like that I'm running loose.

I better go somewhere else, in case she comes back.

I have heard Miss Krause tell the children: *If you are ever lost, whether in the mall or outdoors, stay where you are and someone will find you a lot easier than if you're moving.*

Of course, I'm not lost—Twitch is. Twitch hasn't heard Miss Krause's advice, and he's definitely moving around. So maybe I should stay in one place and watch for Twitch. I wonder: should I go back to the side curtain where Twitch and I were hiding when we first got here?

Too many feet, I think. But before I can decide on somewhere else, I hear something I recognize. Molly in the orchestra (Molly likes series books) has just shaken a handbell. For some reason, Miss Krause and Mr. Ziegler have decided this high jingly note is the sound of magic. It means the Fairy Godmother (Vanessa) and her assistant (Raj) have come onstage. They both love fantasy books—the longer, the better—so these are the perfect roles for them.

With the help of Molly shaking her handbell, and with singing and dancing while twirling a long sparkly cloth that hides people coming onto the stage from backstage, and with a fancy dress that fastens with two easy snaps, and with Marc (who reads mysteries) backstage knocking two blocks of wood together to sound like horses' hooves, and with glitter thrown into the air (in spite of the custodian's grumbling when Miss Krause told him this was the plan), the Fairy Godmother will grant Cinderella's wish to go to the ball.

But the best part of the magic will be that Liam will turn into the rat coachman who will take Cinderella to meet the prince.

I can't miss this, so I quickly settle on a hiding place. There is a piano—not the one in the orchestra, but a smaller one that will be used onstage during the scene at the ball. Mr. Ziegler has given everyone strict instructions not to touch this piano, including Kai, who is meant to be one of the court musicians and is supposed to *pretend* to play it. "Just move your hands over the keys," Mr. Ziegler has told him, "but don't press down, because then random notes would play."

If the keys are not moving on the outside, that means they won't be moving on the inside (Miss Krause once read out loud and showed the children pictures from a book about musical instruments), so they won't knock me around. The lid is open, and the piano is right by the curtain, waiting to be wheeled in for the next scene, so I'll be able to watch the part with the rat. Then I can climb back out before the ball starts.

Kai is sitting on the piano bench reading a graphic novel (always his first choice), so he doesn't see me climb the curtain, then jump into the piano.

I'll be safe here.

Twitch:
Magic

From my hiding spot behind the painted trees and walls, I can hear the children looking for me. I'm prepared to run from behind one piece of cardboard to another to escape them, but the children aren't looking very carefully, so I don't need to find a new hiding place. I have seen children playing *hide-and-seek* on the playground, and they usually do a better job of seeking. I suspect they don't really want to find me. They know Miss Krause shouldn't make a pet of me, so they are letting me get away.

But I can't just get away: I need to find Sweetie,

and I need to do a better job of seeking than the children are doing.

"Sweetie!" I call once the children have, yet again, given up looking. I listen in case he squeaks softly, and I hear someone onstage ask, "Is that, perchance, a rat?"

Oh, no! They've found Sweetie, and they'll take him back to the library, and now he won't get a chance to see the ending of the play, where it finally becomes a happy story. All he'll have seen is the mean and sad parts.

I scurry forward to peek around the curtain at the children playing the play. The Cinderella girl is there, and another girl I haven't seen before, and a boy. Both the new girl and the boy have wings like giant butterflies, except they aren't real wings but are made of sparkly cloth.

Cinderella is holding a tiny cage. "Yes, Fairy Godmother," Cinderella says. "This is a rat. But he's a nice rat. A friendly rat. Every time my stepmother catches him, *I* let him go."

Nice and *friendly* sounds like Sweetie. And *let him go* sounds like a very good way to treat a nice and friendly rat. But as soon as Cinderella opens the cage, I can see what my nose has been telling me all along but I've been in too much of a tizzy to listen: that isn't Sweetie. It isn't a real rat at all, but a toy one.

This, I realize, is the part of the play Sweetie wanted

to see: where the rat hero saves the day. And he's missing it!

I will watch very closely, I decide, so I can tell him every little bit of what I see and hear.

"I mean your rat no harm," the Fairy Godmother girl says. She pulls the toy rat out of the cage and sets it on the ground, then says, "My assistant will help me create magic."

There's a whole bunch of dancing around with a long sparkly cloth, and another boy steps out from behind the back curtain. He stuffs the toy rat in his pocket, then keeps moving so the cloth hides him from the parents watching the play.

Just as the song ends, Cinderella, Fairy Godmother, and Assistant let go of the cloth and it flutters to the floor. At the same time, the new boy tosses a handful of sparkles into the air, so that the pieces slowly drift down around him.

Now everyone can see the new boy. He is dressed all in white, which matches the fur of the toy rat. As well as Sweetie. Wherever he is.

Just in case anybody doesn't understand that he is the rat magically turned into a person, the boy licks his hands and washes his face, just as Sweetie does with his paws.

Oh, I wish Sweetie could be here!

Cinderella claps her hands and acts surprised, even though she had to see the toy rat/boy switch.

The parents watching the play clap, too.

"Cinderella," the Fairy Godmother says, "meet the driver of your coach."

The new boy bows.

There's a lot more singing and dancing and tossing of sparkles, and Fairy Godmother says she's made a coach out of a pumpkin, and horses out of mice. I think pumpkin seeds would be a very fine snack just about now, as my tummy is totally, totally empty, and has been for forever now. But I can see where Fairy Godmother is pointing: back behind the curtain where Sweetie and I first came onstage, and there's no coach, no horses, no pumpkin, and no mice. This magic is even more pretend than turning a boy into a rat.

There's more singing and dancing and tossing of sparkles, and Cinderella gets a new dress and some see-through shoes.

Cinderella gasps. "Glass slippers!"

That doesn't sound sensible. Glass breaks. Glass is not allowed on the playground for fear a child will get hurt. How can someone wear glass shoes?

But Cinderella just goes ahead and puts the new shoes on, clearly not worried about safety.

The new boy, the one who used to be a rat, holds his arm out for her to take hold of.

He must be worried that the glass will be slippery, like the windows I look through when I want to see into the school—the windows that, if I try to climb, I slide down.

"Just don't forget," Fairy Godmother tells Cinderella, "the magic will fade away at midnight. So you must leave by the final stroke of the clock."

"I will, Fairy Godmother," Cinderella assures her. "Thank you so much for everything."

The cloth wall curtains that close from the sides start to close as the children out front play music that sounds like the magic song, but without the singing. Fairy Godmother and Assistant blow kisses and wave goodbye as Cinderella and the coachman who used to be a rat head off toward where Fairy Godmother has said a coach is waiting.

So the play is over. This is the happy ending, with the rat taking Cinderella to the ball so she can meet the prince and get away from Stepmother and the Stepsisters. This is the reason Sweetie loves this story.

And he wasn't here to see it.

Getting Sweetie to the play, to see the rat be the hero—this was my quest.

And I have failed.

I am a failure as a friend.

Sweetie: The Ball

My plan was to climb out of the piano as soon as the scene with the rat coachman (yay, rat coachman!) ended, but the scene hasn't ended yet, and Kai stands up and places his graphic novel in the piano bench. He's standing by the piano, ready to wheel it onto the stage.

Now I can't leave without showing myself.

Ainsley in her going-to-the-ball costume and Liam in his rat coachman costume walk off the stage and into the wings.

I wave at Liam, but not so that he can see me. Still, we rats have to stick together.

Kai wheels the piano onto the stage, but off to the side where the court musicians will play their instruments. Other children, wearing their ballroom finery, bring out the thrones for the royal family and set them between two cardboard pillars. Eduardo, Layla, and Victor, wearing their crowns, take their places. The rest of the stage is meant to be the ballroom floor.

There is clapping, which means the curtains must have opened on the ball scene.

I huddle in the inside of the piano where I can't be seen. Nothing in here is moving, which shows that Kai has remembered not to really press the keys.

Everything is going well.

I have seen the children practice dancing in the library, and I picture them in their costumes dancing on the stage that is decorated to look like a room in the castle.

There's a thump.

Has one of the dancing children fallen over?

The music skitter-screeches to a stop.

Has one of the orchestra members fallen over?

I hope no one is hurt.

I hear Layla announce in her most queenly voice, "And once we have our son settled, we'll need to do some serious repairs on this old castle."

That is not a line from the play. Most likely one of the children working backstage has tripped over something, or maybe some piece of furniture has fallen over. Layla is trying to pretend everything is fine, and in another moment Mr. Ziegler must also decide to pretend that everything is fine, because I hear him tap his conducting wand on a music stand, and in another moment the dance music starts again.

I let myself relax.

Until I hear Eduardo give a very un-kingly *"Eeek!"*

Eeek! isn't a someone-or-something-has-fallen-down sound.

For some reason, Twitch comes to my mind.

Twitch:
Still Not Seeing That Ball

Cinderella has met the rat coachman and now she can go visit the prince and live happily ever after. The end. Well, that was nice after all.

Once the curtains meet in the middle, I think that everyone will go home. This will make it easier for me to find Sweetie, since I won't have to worry about Miss Krause hunting for me.

But once the curtain is closed, the children and the

music teacher don't stop playing music. They only start playing different music.

Children flitter and flutter on the stage like birds around a squirrel feeder, the girls in their sparkly skirts and beads, and the boys with their jackets with the gleaming buttons and their pants with their shiny stripes. Some of the girls and boys move furniture around, including the small piano I saw before, and then they all start dancing.

Maybe the play isn't over after all.

I will need to continue to look for Sweetie even with everyone still here, even if they are getting in my way.

The curtains pull apart once more, and the parents clap.

King and Queen and Prince are sitting on big chairs that are higher up and close to the back curtain so that they can see the dancers. Queen asks Prince, "Are you enjoying the ball?"

Prince yawns.

I don't blame him. I can't see the ball, either. There is no throwing, kicking, bouncing, or dodging. Just dancing.

Prince pulls out a book and begins to read.

I wonder if it is the story of Cinderella. Maybe he is reading ahead to get to the happy ending.

What I need, I decide, is a high-squirrel view of the stage. I don't want to climb the curtain walls because I

don't have time for hide-and-seek with Miss Krause. What else can I climb where I won't been seen?

I notice that tall pieces of cardboard have been set up

behind where King, Queen, and Prince are sitting. They look like the cardboard trees I hid behind backstage, but someone forgot to paint bark—or branches. All I need to do is climb one and I'll have a squirrel's-eye view of the whole stage area. Wherever Sweetie is, I'll be able to see him.

I jump onto the back of one of those not-tree trees.

But a not-tree isn't nearly as steady as a *tree.*

It rocks.

It sways.

It tips.

It falls behind where King and Queen and Prince are sitting.

Thump!

Maybe nobody will notice.

King says, *"Eeek!"*

Queen gives a startled jump and glances behind her.

Prince gets on his knees on the seat of the chair to look. But I've already run behind the side curtain.

The music and the dancing and any ball-playing that might be going on stop. The parents gasp, and then there is total silence.

Into that silence Queen tells King, "And once we have our son settled, we'll need to do some serious repairs on this old castle."

"Yes, my dear," King agrees.

The music teacher taps his stick on a music stand, and the music starts once more. So does the dancing. I've given up hoping for ball-playing.

I look around for something else to climb.

Well, there are those big chairs they're sitting on . . .

I climb up the leg of the middle one, then jump onto the back part.

When I land, King gives a second, even louder *"Eeek!"*

But he can't see me clinging to his chair behind him, and Queen and Prince only look, once again, down at the fallen not-tree, not at the back of King's chair.

I climb as far as I can go up the back of the chair. All I can see is chair-back.

King is wearing a stiff gold-colored hat with points on it. I'm wondering if he's likely to notice if I climb onto that so I can face any direction I want to be facing without the chair-back being in the way.

But just then something catches my attention: something small and white and furry, peeking out from inside the piano onstage, the one that is there for the pretend music. The lid is up, and I can see that Sweetie is peeking out from inside, looking around with his not-very-strong red eyes. His strong pink nose wiggles as he tries to sniff out what is going on.

He *has* been able to see the play, first from backstage, and now from the stage itself.

Yay! I haven't failed at the quest. I haven't failed at being a friend.

I jump off the back of King's chair and run to where Sweetie and I were first standing. Once the boy wheels the piano backstage, Sweetie and I will be together again.

The Cinderella girl and Prince have found each other, and Prince is no longer bored. They dance and sing until

Cinderella suddenly says, "Oh my goodness! Is that the clock bonging midnight? I hate to run, but: goodbye!"

The sometimes-a-rat coachman is in the audy-toy-room where the parents are sitting, and he is waving for her to come, to hurry.

"But—" Prince says.

Cinderella runs down the stairs from the stage. Then she and Coachman run up the path between the chairs so fast, Cinderella runs right out of one of her glass shoes. I *knew* they were a mistake!

Coachman takes her arm and they run out the back door, where Sweetie and I first came in. *Yay!* for the rat coachman saving Cinderella! I'm not sure what he just saved her from, but *Yay!*

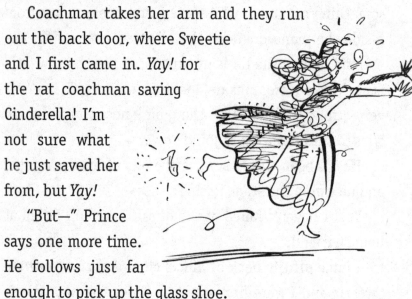

"But—" Prince says one more time. He follows just far enough to pick up the glass shoe.

Will he put it on?

He doesn't.

Instead, he goes back up onstage to his chair and sits, staring at the shoe. Probably thinking: *Glass shoe. What a bad idea!*

Slowly, the curtains come in from the sides again, meeting in the middle, making most of the stage once more into backstage.

Sweetie:
At the Stroke of Midnight

There are no more alarming sounds from the stage or from backstage as the ballroom scene continues.

Was it Twitch, but now he's stopped what he was doing? Or do I just have a worries-about-too-many-things mind?

I think I can make out Miss Krause off in the wings. All I can see is a blob, but she's a taller blob than the children, so I believe it's her. And she isn't running around or having the backstage children running around, so—even if it was Twitch causing the commotion—he must be well hidden now.

I decide I, too, need to be well hidden before Miss Krause sees me, so I draw my head back into the inside of the piano.

But I peek out as often as I dare.

Ainsley enters the ballroom dressed in her beautiful ballroom gown. Victor leaves his throne to dance with her. Mr. Ziegler has said that the audience will be able to tell by the music that they are falling in love. I wonder if Molly will ring the handbell that is a sign of magic happening, but she doesn't need to.

We have the rat coachman to thank for all of this.

Then, all of a sudden, Molly is ringing a second handbell, a great big one that goes *Gong! Gong! Gong!*

That is Cinderella's signal that she should leave, and she runs offstage, joining a white blob—probably the coachman—waiting to run her up the aisle and to the back door before the clock strikes twelve.

Even though I know how the story goes, I'm so excited I forget to count. But they must make it out in time because Molly rings the bell two more times after the door closes behind them.

Beyond the closed doors, there's the sound of a crash. I know this is part of the play, but it startles me, and I can't help it. I think: *Twitch!*

But I know it's not Twitch. It's supposed to be the coach crashing as it turns back into a pumpkin. Several of the boys have been sent to stand outside the auditorium and now they make neighing sounds like horses, then squeaking sounds, which are the horses changing back to mice. (Never having met a horse, I don't know how the boys do at neighing, but I know they sound nothing at all like mice.)

Still, I breathe a sigh of relief and snuggle way down into the piano.

Very soon the audience claps, and I feel the piano move as Kai wheels *my* coach offstage to get ready for the play's last act.

I climb out of the piano while no one is looking. I hope to see Twitch safe and sound so we can watch the end of the play together.

I spot him—but Miss Krause is standing right behind him.

"Twitch!" I warn.

Not in time.

"Got you!" Miss Krause says.

Twitch: Trapped!

I watch as the piano with Sweetie in it is wheeled off the stage.

So . . . is *this* the happy ending for the play? The rat coachman has brought Cinderella to where she said—well, *sang*—was the one place in the whole world she wanted to go. She danced with the prince, which made the prince happy even though people-dancing does not involve nearly so much leaping up into the air as squirrel-dancing does. And she left before the clock stopped bonging, which was what Fairy Godmother and

Assistant told her she must do, so they should be happy, too.

I am ready for my own happy ending, which means reuniting with Sweetie and making sure he gets back to the library.

But I am remembering I've already thought before that the play was finished being played, and it wasn't.

And, sure enough, it isn't over now, either.

Yes, the curtains have closed. And Prince, King, Queen, and all the dancers start moving furniture to the sides of backstage (including the piano with Sweetie in it). But now from out front there is a sound like a crash (not me, really!), and this is followed by I-don't-know-what-they-are sounds.

I dart among all those quickly moving feet backstage and peek beneath the curtain to see what is happening on the other side.

The Cinderella girl has returned to the little bit of stage in front of the curtain, and she starts singing that her beautiful dress has turned back to rags, and that the coach is gone, and that the horses are once again mice and the coachman a rat. (That's a relief! I didn't even know to worry about the rat being stuck as a human!) She sings that she is happy because she has her memories of this one magical night, and she even has one glass slipper to keep, just in case she ever starts to think this was all only a dream.

Okay, so surely *this* is the happy ending.

But not for me.

Thunk! The lights go out. Someone has just dropped something over me. I suspect, by the plastic smell of it, that it's one of those small garbage cans that the people keep in every classroom.

And, apparently, they keep them backstage, too.

"Got you!" I recognize Miss Krause's voice. She slides the can—and me with it!—across the floor fast enough that

I have to scurry or sweep the floor with my belly. "Marc!" Miss Krause calls. "Get over here."

"Yes, Miss Krause?" a boy answers, in the timid voice of someone who is worried that he's been caught doing something he shouldn't.

Miss Krause says, "Sit on this trash can. I finally caught that squirrel, and I don't want it getting loose until the custodian can take it for a long ride far enough away so it can't ever find its way back in."

Away? Away from my tree in the schoolyard where I live?

The boy she's been talking to says, "Okay, Miss Krause," and sits on the upturned trash can. He lets his feet dangle, banging against the side, which will eventually make my head hurt, but meanwhile I have more important things to think about.

Very, very important things.

It's too dark to see in here. But my nose still works. What my nose knows is that the trash can wasn't completely empty when Miss Krause upended it. Someone has thrown pistachio nuts away, and they got dragged along with me! I sniff them out in the darkness. I am guessing, by the way the shells are completely closed in, that whoever had these wasn't able to open them. But squirrel teeth are stronger than people teeth.

I haven't eaten in soooo loooong, and pistachios are my favorite food!

There will be time to think about how to escape once I've gobbled them all down.

But after I've finished eating the nuts, I notice a strange thing: I can still hear chewing. Is it so dark that I've gotten confused? I raise my paw to my mouth to see if my jaw is still moving.

Nope.

I go to where the chewing noise is coming from. I sniff. Sweetie!

Sweetie is outside the trash can and he's chewing the plastic.

"Sweetie!" I call out.

"Twitch!" he calls back.

I start chewing, too.

In another moment, a crack appears in the plastic, which lets in light. I see sharp little rat teeth and a little pink rat nose.

The boy Miss Krause set on the trash can continues to

swing his legs, banging his heels against the side, so he doesn't feel our chewing.

Sweetie chews where he's chewing and I chew where I'm chewing, and in not too much time at all we've formed a hole big enough for me to wriggle out of.

I wish I had known to save a pistachio for him.

"Yay!" I say. "You rescued me!"

"Yay!" Sweetie agrees. "I was hiding in the piano backstage where I could see everything and then, Twitch, they wheeled the piano right *onstage,* and I could see even more!"

"Yay!" I say again, even though I already knew this. "That means you played in the play!"

And he repeats "Yay!" too. Then he says, "But I saw Miss Krause capture you." His nose wiggles. "Maybe we should go back to the library now."

I don't believe he really wants to leave until the play is over. Good friends can sense these things. I tell him, "We just need a new place to hide." I glance around. "I'm sure to come up with a plan," I say. "I always have good plans."

Sweetie:
Last Act

"Maybe we've had enough plans," I tell Twitch.

"Nonsense!" he tells me. "Ooo, let's go up onto this table."

He's talking about the prop table, where small things are kept that are used in the play, things like Cinderella's dusting cloth, brushes and combs and necklaces for the stepsisters, the lute with the broken string, the toy rat that was the coachman before Liam was the coachman.

I'm huffing a bit from trying to keep up with Twitch on the climb. "Under this dusting cloth?" I ask.

Twitch lifts the cover off a box. "No, here. They won't be using this again."

There are bunched-up pieces of cloth to keep the glass slipper from rattling around, but I can see how Twitch would think there's room for both of us.

I balance on the edge of the box. "No, wait," I squeak. "They *will* be using this—"

But one of the children is walking straight toward us. Twitch shoves, and I fall into the box. Twitch lets the cover drop. He's probably hiding behind or underneath something else on the prop table. He's probably planning to climb into the box once the boy has passed by.

Except the boy *doesn't* pass by. I knew he wouldn't because I know what this box with one glass slipper in it is for.

The boy picks up the box with me in it. And carries me onstage.

Twitch:
Curtain Call

Oops!

Maybe, I think as I watch the boy carrying away the box with Sweetie in it, *the play is over and they're taking everything back to the library.*

Except the curtains are still open, showing Stepmother and Stepsisters.

A boy with a metal tube blows into it to make some musical notes. Then the boy with the box with Sweetie in it steps into the room and tells Stepmother and Stepsisters, "His Royal Highness the prince has decreed that every maid in the kingdom shall try on this shoe until we find she who left it behind at the ball. She whom it fits will be his royal bride."

Which I guess means he'll be opening the box onstage. Double oops!

I jump down from the table where the box used to be, to stand closer to the curtain. I watch as the stepsisters rush up to the boy who is holding the box.

"Oooo, me first! Me first!" one of the stepsisters says, but the other one nudges her out of the way and dangles her foot in front of the boy.

The boy kneels at her feet and reaches in to pull out the glass shoe. Sweetie must be crouched in a corner, because the boy doesn't see him. The boy balances the glass shoe on Stepsister's toes and announces, "Your feet are too big."

"Are not!" she says. "This shoe is too small!"

The other stepsister pushes ahead. "Me! Me!"

Again, the shoe doesn't go all the way on.

"Are there no more young maids in the house?" the boy asks.

"No!" Stepmother says.

"No!" Stepsister One says.

"No!" Stepsister Two says.

"It's just"—the boy sighs—"this is the last house."

"Sorry."

"Nuh-uh."

"Those are the breaks. Want to try my foot again?"

Cinderella runs in. "Someone," she announces, "locked me in the attic!"

I wonder if it was Miss Krause, since she's the one who trapped me under the trash can.

"Well, let me try the glass slipper on you," says the boy with the glass shoe.

He slips it over her toes and around her heel.

"Yay!" the parents in the audy-toy-room cheer.

"Boo!" the stepsisters call back.

To show how upset she is, one of them kicks the box the shoe came in.

The box tips over.
And
   out
      rolls
         Sweetie.

The boy with the tube doesn't notice and he blows some more musical notes, but he's drowned out by Stepmother screaming, *"Eeek!"*

Stepsister One screeches, "It's a mouse!"

Stepsister Two corrects her: "It's a *rat.*"

The stepsisters clutch each other and scream.

They all take big steps back, including Glass-Slipper Boy and Tube Boy.

Parents in the audy-toy-room stand, ready to rush forward if their children need rescuing.

Cinderella swoops in and picks up Sweetie. "Don't be alarmed," she tells all: the boy who put the shoe on her foot, the other boy with the musical tube, the stepmother and stepsisters, the parents. "This is Sweetie. From the library. Which is in"—she gestures toward the back of the audy-toy-room—"the other part of the house. He's very friendly. All the boys and girls know him." She's scratching the top of his head with her finger, and Sweetie makes the clicking noise he makes when he is very, very happy.

Prince steps forward. "I heard the trumpet fanfare," he says. "Has my true love been found?"

"Yes, Your Highness," says the boy who brought the shoe. "Your true love and her pet rat."

"Well, that's . . . wonderful," Prince says.

Cinderella pulls the second glass shoe from her pocket and slips that on, while Prince and the three step-people pet Sweetie, now that they recognize him.

The boy with the musical tube blows it again, then announces: "And they all lived happily ever after: Cinderella and the prince and the rat."

The children bow, more music is played, the parents clap, and all the children who were in the play come forward—including the Marc boy, who is supposed to be guarding me in the trash can—and even Miss Krause. They all bow together. Then the curtain that went up when the play first began comes down and finally, *finally* the play is really, truly finished.

The children who were onstage climb down the stairs or jump off the stage, and the parents squeeze in around them like ants on a spilled juice box.

The Cinderella girl is getting the most attention. That's because she's holding Sweetie. Some of the parents ask if they can pet him, and she says they may, but only if they are very gentle.

The parents tell Miss Krause things like:

"Such fun!"

"That was so clever of you to use real animals."

And "They stole the show."

Miss Krause says, "Hmmm."

She waits for the parents to leave, then she leans in and tells Sweetie, "You are a star. I'm so sorry. I must not have closed your cage properly this afternoon, but I'm glad you found us and that you're safe." She scratches between his ears. "You don't happen to be friends with a squirrel, do you?"

Sweetie is looking very happy. I know he can't see me, not with his weak eyes, but then he raises a paw toward the stage to wave at me.

I still think that the best part of the play was the popcorn at the beginning, but I am caught up in the excitement. Even though nobody is facing the stage anymore so no one can see me, I run to stand in front of the curtain.

I bow, as the children did. "Once upon a time," I say, using my *big* voice, "I had a friend named Sweetie, and we went on a quest to see a play together. We traveled vast distances and overcame great obstacles. We had adventures and escapes and food to eat. Sweetie got to play in the play. And I got to take a bow afterward. And a good friend is even better than an acorn."

I take another bow, looking forward to telling Sweetie my new story tomorrow.

Being a squirrel with a good friend is the best thing in the world.

Afterword:
Class Pets Talk About Plays

SWEETIE, THE LIBRARY RAT:

A play is a story that is acted out. A play can take place anywhere: in a classroom, in a backyard, on a stage—even in a rat's cage in the library. When a play is acted out in a school, often that's in an auditorium with a stage.

A stage can have—but it doesn't *need* to have—curtains. Curtains can be opened from the middle to the sides, or they can go up. They are used to keep the audience from seeing the backstage area where the stage crew, or helpers, might be moving around scenery or furniture to set up for the next part of the play. Or curtains might be opened or closed to mark the end of a scene.

Often there are curtains on the sides, which are called the wings, and these curtains don't open. Here squirrels and rats can watch the play while being pretty much not seen and out of the way IF THEY DON'T MOVE!

Ahem.

It's also where actors may wait before it's their turn to go onstage, or where stage crew members are busy operating lights or handing out props before an actor goes onstage. Sometimes actors change their costumes in the wings. This is where the stage manager (who is like the play boss, like Miss Krause) keeps an eye on what's going on so that things move smoothly.

Unless, of course, a squirrel is involved.

GREEN EGGS AND HAMSTER, FIRST-GRADE HAMSTER:

Story + actors + stage = a play.

Play + students = fun!

Play + students + squirrel = chaos!

Backstage is the part of the stage that the audience can't see.

Upstage is the part of the stage closest to the back curtains, which are never opened because they hide things not being used for the play.

Downstage is the part of the stage closest to the audience.

Sometimes there is an **apron**, which is the part of downstage in front of all the curtains. Actors might stand here for a quick scene that doesn't need any scenery.

To figure out **stage left** and **stage right**, think of yourself as the actor facing the audience. Now stretch both arms out to your sides. Your left hand (or paw, if you're a hamster) is pointing **stage left**, and your right hand or paw is pointing **stage right**.

Upstage + downstage + stage left + stage right = onstage.

But if you've been running around in your hamster wheel, these directions might wobble and change.

MISS LUCY COTTONTAIL, SECOND-GRADE RABBIT:

I am not stuck-up, the way that squirrel says I am, but I know I would be good at acting in a play. I am smart, and I am cute. And I don't run around making a nuisance of myself the way certain squirrels do.

Usually, actors have to try out for a play in an audition, where they read lines from the play, or sing a song if there are songs in the play, or dance if there is dancing.

I would have made a great Cinderella, but nobody told me when the audition was.

A SCHOOL OF NEON TETRAS, THIRD-GRADE FISH:

We are a school in a school.

That idea tickles us.

The idea of a play does not tickle us.

We play by swimming in our pond, which is surrounded by glass. We swim around the things in our pond: the shipwreck and the miniature man with a treasure chest that opens and closes. We swim over the sparkly stones on the floor of our square pond.

We ignore the catfish, who keeps the glass of our pond clean.

This is all the play we need, for we are a school in a school.

LENORE, FOURTH-GRADE PARROT:

¡Hola! I have made up a poem for the occasion.

A play is a bunch of words
acted out by kids or birds.
The words tell a story,
but the best category—
—reading or writing, performing or rehearsing—
are plays told through versing.

Okay, okay! I know it's that poem that needs more rehearsing.

NANCY, ART ROOM TURTLE:

Art is very important in plays because someone needs to decorate the stage so that people can tell where the play is happening. Where a story is happening can be very important. This can be done with furniture, but it also includes painting backdrops that show scenery: inside walls, outside walls, forest, classroom, castle, cave, art gallery. The scenery could even be painted to look like the glass case where I live, with water and a dry area and a food bowl, and my heat lamp.

Lovely heat lamp, making me warm and cozy. Mmmmm . . .

Oops, sorry, I dozed off there for a moment.

Costumes are part of the setting, too. Sometimes actors are able to use their own clothing; sometimes special clothes need to be bought or made, and that's a kind of art as well.

Turtles don't need clothes. We wear our shells. Those should never—ever!—be painted or decorated with beads and stickers.

All this talking has made me tired. I think I'll take a nap under my nice heat lamp . . . Mmmmm . . .

ANGEL, FIFTH-GRADE CORN SNAKE:

Sassafras! (Isn't that a simply sensational morsel of a word!)

Speaking of *sensational*, plays are a sensational example of a school society sharing in something amusing as well as scholarly.

Those students participating expand their skills and self-confidence, simultaneously instilling satisfaction in the assembled spectators.

Should I be asked, I'd certainly embrace the possibility of starring in a show. May I be so brassy as to suggest a story I've been scripting called SNAKES ARE STUPENDOUS.

GALILEO AND NEWTON, SCIENCE LAB GECKOS:

GALILEO: Plays are written in script form.

NEWTON: That means just the words
words that people say.

GALILEO: So, no description—

NEWTON: —no thoughts—

GALILEO: —no "Once upon a time—"

NEWTON: —or "And then they lived
happily ever after."

GALILEO: I already covered that
when I said what I said.

NEWTON: I made it clearer.

GALILEO: No, you didn't. You just added words.

NEWTON: To make it clearer.

GALILEO: Even though it was already clear
enough.

NEWTON: Maybe. Maybe not.

GALILEO: We think the best plays are set
in science labs.

NEWTON: The fun and drama of—

GALILEO: —baking-soda-and-vinegar volcanoes that actually erupt!

NEWTON: I was going to say that.

GALILEO: I said it first.

NEWTON: I can say it, too: baking-soda-and-vinegar volcanoes that actually erupt!

GALILEO: Kind of pointless now.

NEWTON: There's also—

GALILEO: —Lego rubber-band cars—

NEWTON: —which can go shooting off in unexpected directions—

GALILEO: —paper airplane tossing—

NEWTON: Talk about unexpected directions!

GALILEO: —and exploding Peeps in a microwave.

NEWTON: I don't know why there aren't more plays set in science labs.

GALILEO: It's a mystery.

NEWTON   I just said that.

GALILEO: No, you said that *you* didn't know. *Mystery* shows that lots of people don't know.

NEWTON: You always have to have the last word, don't you?

GALILEO: Not always.

NEWTON: Usually.

GALILEO: *Usually* doesn't mean *always*.

NEWTON: You're doing it again.

GALILEO: No, I'm not.

NEWTON: You are.

GALILEO: Not.

TWITCH, THE SCHOOLYARD SQUIRREL:

Being in a play with my friend Sweetie was lots of fun. Sweetie tells me that when actors want to wish fun and luck to one another, what they say is *Break a leg.* This sounds like the opposite of fun and luck to me, but Sweetie usually knows what he's talking about.

I wonder how actors wish luck to a snake?

Anyway, now that I know everything there is to know about plays, I still think the best part is the snacks.

CUDDLES, THE PRINCIPAL'S DOG:

Dumb squirrel

Read more books about Twitch and his adventures!

Nominated for seven state awards!

"A whole lot of fun." —*Kirkus Reviews*

"(A) fun read . . . and a good read-aloud."
—*School Library Journal*

SQUIRREL
— IN THE —
HOUSE

BY
Vivian Vande Velde

ILLUSTRATED BY
Steve Björkman

"This is a story young readers will love."
—*School Library Journal*

"Delightfully nutty chapter-book fare."
—*Kirkus Reviews*

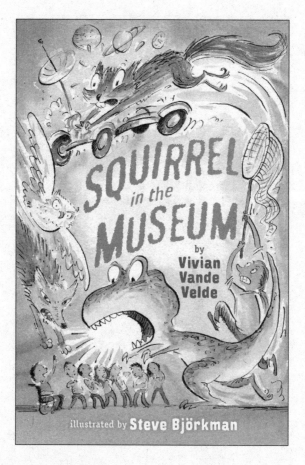

"When a reader requests a short, funny chapter book, hope that this one's on the shelf."—*Booklist*

"Readers . . . might even learn a little science as they follow his museum adventures."
—*School Library Connection*

A Conversation with Vivian Vande Velde

Q: What was the inspiration behind Inside *8 Class Pets + 1 Squirrel & 1 Dog = Chaos*? Is any part of it based on actual events from your past?

A: No actual events. It's just that I love seeing those accounts about bonds of friendship between unlikely pairs—particularly interspecies friends, and most especially between animals that you would normally not expect to be nurturing to each other: Koko the gorilla hugging her pet kitten, All Ball; an elephant and a dog playing together; a fawn licking a cat; a zoo tiger raising piglets along with her own cubs. If you do an internet search on "unusual animal friends," you'll see all sorts of things to make you go "Awww!"

(You absolutely need to go to YouTube and type in "dog, cat, rat"!)

So I decided I wanted to write about a whole group of animals working together.

Q: We noticed you attribute different styles of writing to each animal's personality. How did you decide what was best for each?

A: Some seemed obvious, such as that the school of tetras would speak with one voice ("We are in a school in a school. . . .") and that their viewpoint would be the most limited (and that they don't even realize this) since they cannot leave their tank.

If you've ever seen a hamster go round and round in a hamster wheel, you HAVE to have had the thought, "How can he not get dizzy?" So the hamster in my story is dizzy, but I didn't want that to translate to dumb. So he's very mathematical. (Except, of course, after he's been on the hamster wheel; then the numbers on the clock move and become hard to count.)

The parrot is from South America, so she has a bit of

an accent. I also decided she'd have the soul of a poet. Perhaps not a very good poet, but still, poetry is very subjective, so who are we to criticize?

Since the geckos keep interrupting each other and finishing one another's sentences, it immediately became obvious that their chapter should be written all in dialogue, as in a script. And that each one would always try to get in the last word.

Q: Was it difficult writing from the perspectives of various animals?

A: More fun than difficult to try to give each a unique voice.

Q: Out of all of the characters in the book, which one do you relate to the most?

A: Ooo, I always relate to all my characters (even the villains). But I guess I'm closest to Sweetie, the library rat, who loves books and who sees himself in the stories he hears. So he thinks the hero of the Cinderella story is the rat, because without the rat being turned into a coachman, Cinderella would never get to the ball.

Q: Did you work with the illustrator on how you wanted the illustrations to look?

A: I did not work with Steve Björkman at all—but aren't his illustrations full of fun and energy?!

Q: Do you have any pets of your own?

A: At the moment, my husband and I have one cat, Alf (named after the cat-eating alien in the TV series from the 1980s because they're the same color and just about as silly).